# Naughty Bus

by Jan and Jerry Oke

Post Production by Tony Swinney.  Designed by Fergus Fleming and Olaf Liunberg.

For
Jessica, Kiernan, Frances, Arthur, Helen and Jack.

Published by: Little Knowall Publishing,
9 Little Knowle, Budleigh Salterton, Devon EX9 6QS.

First Edition: September 2004
Revised Edition: March 2005
Reprinted: September 2006
Revised Edition: August 2007
Reprinted: June 2010

ISBN 978-0-9547921-1-4

Printed in England by Hampton Printing (Bristol) Ltd.

This is for you.

I hope you're a good driver.

# It's a bus!
# Let's play!!!

Did you say

"thankyou"?

I'm a London bus.

buildings

are tall

and

there's

lots of

traffic.

# People wait at the

ous stop.

But when
I'm full up,

I drive

*straight past them!*

Hey Mr Bus Driver! Come to the table.

I have an
IMPORTANT
job to do.

I must take
my passengers
where they
want to go.

# And nothing must

# stand in my way!!!!!!!

Hold very tight please.

Ding ding.

What a mess! You can get down from the table now.

Shoo! Shoo! Into the garden with you!

I don't think much of the roads around here.

What's that over there?

It's a pond. And I can see my reflection in it.

I am definitely the most handsome bus I know.

Just a little bit closer........................

Too close!

And now I'm
the silliest bus
I know.

I can't swim

Oh what shall I do? It's so cold down here and lonely too.

I want my boy! Don't forget me!

Don't leave me here all alone.

# Don't worry bus.

# The rescue

ruck will save you.

I'll let down my hoo
winch will soon
pull you out.

Thank you for saving me.

# k and my **powerful**

I didn't mean to
be naughty.

And I promise
I won't play on
my own near
the water again,

Can we go
home now?

Soon we'll be tucked up cosy in bed.

But first
we need
to wash.

Nobody
lo♥es a
dirty bus.

And don't forget to

brush your teeth.

# Good night.

# Sleep tight.

# Sometimes I'm a night bus.